What If?

A Novella

Stuart Harvey

This is a work of fiction. Names, characters, businesses, places, events and incidents are either the products of the author's imagination or used in a fictitious manner. Any resemblance to actual persons, living or dead, or actual events is purely coincidental.

Other books by Stuart Harvey

The Charlie Sayer Trilogy

Crossing the Line (2012)

Blood Route (2018)

You See (2020)

Dedicated to all those mental health professionals who make themselves available to help those who need someone to listen when they have something to say.

All royalties from the sale of the paperback and hardback editions of this book are being donated to PAPYRUS a UK charity that is dedicated to the prevention of suicide and the promotion of positive mental health and emotional wellbeing in young people.

They deserve our support.

"In a world where you can be anything, be kind."

Caroline Flack

"Suicide is a serious thing. And if you know anyone who is suicidal, you need to get them help. No one should be in pain. Everyone should love themselves."

Gerard Way

"Psychological illnesses can be fixed if sorted out early enough. We've got to keep the issue at the forefront of people's minds ... just talking about it makes all the difference."

Prince Harry, Duke of Sussex

Remembering some of those whose suicide meant that they went too soon

Molly Russell. Student. Died November 2017, age 14.

Ellie Soutter. Athlete. Died July 25, 2018, age 18.

Sylvia Plath. Poet. Died February 11, 1963, age 30.

Kurt Cobain. Musician. Died April 5, 1994, age 27.

Caroline Flack. Presenter. Died February 15, 2020, age 40

Stuart Adamson. Musician. Died December 16 2001, age 43.

Robin Williams. Actor. Died August 11, 2014, age 63.

Alexander McQueen. Designer. Died February 11, 2010, age 40.

Paula Yates. Presenter. Died September 2000, age 41.

This should make us all stop and think

According to statistics released in the UK by the Samaritans organization, in 2018 (the most recent statistics available at time of publication), there were 6,859 suicides in the United Kingdom and Northern Ireland. That equates to one every hour and a quarter, and was a rise of some 10.9% on the previous year.

Whilst the highest rate is among men within the forty-five to forty-nine years of age range, suicides in that year of young people under the age of twenty-five, showed the biggest increase and that was 23.7%.

One

Friday at last! Oh, how he loved Fridays.

For sure, Fridays signaled the start of the weekend, but more importantly they signaled the end of the working week. From around six in the evening on a Friday until maybe nine Sunday evening, he could forget about work. Forget about that bastard of a boss who was forever telling him how his sales were not high enough, how useless he was at selling anyway, and that perhaps he should look for another job. Easier said than done.

Didn't that arsehole Goodman know how tough it was out there to find another job? Of course, he didn't, didn't care either. That's why he could ride the salesmen so hard. Knew they had no choice but to kiss arse, to give in to his rantings and just try and make a living.

And that's what he did all week. But come Friday he could switch off his work mobile and try to forget all about bloody Goodman until he got his suit ready on Sunday evening, ready for Monday and another week.

Shit I need a drink, he thought as he drew away from his last client. His last "No Sale" of another bad week.

Then there it was up ahead. His haven. His personal Shangri La. Well at least for a couple of hours.

Two

The Eildon Hill was just like hundreds if not thousands of other pubs and bars spread across England, in other words unremarkable. Scotsman Rab had taken it over maybe twenty years before when it was The Black Rabbit, a run-down local pub with a regular clientele of less than thirty. But Rab had dreams. So, he bought it, painted the outside, filled the inside with his collection of music memorabilia and re-named it after his favorite Big Country track. Now, to those that frequented it, and they still numbered the wrong side of thirty, it was simply The Hill. Rab's dreams may have given way to a good dose of reality, but his passion for what he had created remained undiminished by low sales.

To those just driving past, The Hill was not a place that immediately grabbed your attention, so few ever stopped. Rab didn't mind though. Although he had spent most of his life savings on the place since taking it over, most of that had gone on filling the inside with more music memorabilia because, when push came to shove, he was a music lover and not an interior designer. In fact, to put it bluntly, he was nuts about music and frankly couldn't give a rat's arse what the outside looked like. If you didn't like the way the pub looked, well he didn't give it a thought. Criticize his memorabilia though, well that was a different proposition, as many first-time visitors found out to their cost.

But as the world's most useless printer cartridge salesman, and that was Godman's description not his own, approached The Hill, life to him seemed just about bloody perfect. The Hill had that effect on him.

The fact that it was also just a mile from his home helped too, because after a few drinks he could safely leave his car in the car park and drag his weary body home, knowing his old banger would still be there the next day when he needed it again. No worries about drink driving for him then.

So, at six thirty on a damp and chilly October, Friday evening, just as the light was beginning to fade, he pulled in to a largely empty car park and smiled. At last, he thought, time for me.

Spirits duly uplifted by the thought of what lay ahead behind the closed door of The Hill, he locked his car, strode across the uneven gravel car park carefully avoiding the puddles that remained after that afternoon's showers, and pushed the door open.

At last, he thought.

Three

Entering the bar, and there was only one, he saw Rab bottling up ready for the Friday night rush, which to Rab meant more than ten customers.

Rab paused his stocking up of the shelves and looked up towards the door to see who had entered.

"Hey HP. How you doin'?" He asked in his best Joey Tribbiani impression. Oh, yes Rab was a mad Friends fan too!

"Shit." Came the reply, "And must you always call me HP?"

"It's Hewlett Packard old mate. You know 'cos you sell printer cartridges." Came the reply.

"Actually, according to my boss, I don't sell them."

Rab laughed, "Bad week?"

"What do you think? Why should this week be any different to all the others?"

Rab nodded and turned towards the shelf that held the beer glasses. He selected one and grabbed a bottle of Brooklyn East India IPA from the cold cabinet. Pulling the cap, he placed the bottle and the beer glass in front of HP and returned to work.

HP liked to pour his own beer. He also loved American IPA especially Brooklyn East India and marveled at how such an iconic beer had found its way to a run-down boozer like The Hill. Still he didn't care. He just drunk the beer and wallowed in its taste.

He poured the first of his beer into the glass, careful not to over fill the glass. He took his first taste, sighed and looked around at the familiar surroundings.

Taking in the long bar and the empty bar stools he counted just one other punter, sat alone in one of the bars half a dozen enclosed booths. Rab had modelled them on a diner he had once visited in upstate New Jersey and the semi-circular booths sported red leather seats and wooden tables that Rab would shine religiously before opening. They could seat five or six people but tonight the only one that was being used housed just one lonely soul, leant forward and nursing a glass tumbler containing a brown liquid and melting ice. He assumed it was whisky.

His eyes dwelt for a while at the guy in the booth and he decided it was not someone he knew. Turning to Rab he asked,

"Who's that?"

"No idea. Came in about an hour ago just as I was opening up. Been drinking Jameson's ever since. Must have had four. Good customer for Friday night."

"Good for here any night." Came the reply accompanied by a laugh.

"Piss off."

Four

HP, as Rab had affectionately called him, was in fact Kenny Jones. He was thirty-five years old, single, with a negative bank account, and living in a bedsit above a fish and chip shop. To anyone who knew him he had zero worth and zero prospects. Sadly, all of his attempts at securing a girlfriend seemed to have been done with girls that also held those opinions. In short, he was single and had been for as long as he could remember. So, drinking IPA at The Hill was his sole vice.

To those that asked, and Rab had been one of them, he would confirm that his long-departed Dad had been a Small Faces fan and named him after their erstwhile drummer. So much of a fan he had been his birth certificate actually had him as Kenny Jones, not Kenneth, simply Kenny.

For his part he had little time for Rod Stewart and the Small Faces, or any of that style of music, preferring instead to listen to jazz.

You would have thought that a love for anything musical would mean that he and Rab had something in common and that this was why he kept coming back to The Hill. Not a bit of it. Rab hated jazz. Said it was just a bunch of guys all playing different tunes together at the same time.

But that didn't stop Kenny from being Rab's best customer by far. Not a bit of it. In fact, Rab saw HP, as he preferred to call him, as a challenge. As a heathen who needed educating in the way of the music world.

Over the years Rab had had some success. Now Kenny actually tolerated Fleetwood Mac, especially from the Peter Green era, and would sometimes listen to some Melody Gardot who was the nearest thing to a jazz come popular music crossover that both satisfied he and Rab.

As he did every time he sat at the bar, Kenny looked around studying the music memorabilia Rab had accumulated and which now adorned every inch of his bar.

Behind the bar was a solid area filled with vinyl album covers from Rab's favourites such as The Eagles, Gram Parsons, Crosby Stills Nash and Young, Jackson Browne and many others who had started life in Laurel Canyon back in the sixties when the Troubadour was the place to go.

Over to the right was another corner with Rab's rock heroes such as Queen, Led Zeppelin, Fleetwood Mac, Dire Straits and Bon Jovi. Then to the left were the females who he adored, Melanie, Carole King, Linda Ronstadt and surprisingly as far as Kenny was concerned, Lady Ga Ga.

Pride of place though belonged to an area not far from where the stranger now sat. That was the Big Country corner.

There Rab's God, Stuart Adamson held court.

Rab had once met the Big Country front man at a concert at Barrowlands Ballroom in Glasgow way back in 1983, when they performed what is widely regarded as the best live gig ever witnessed at this famous auditorium.

Pride of place in this area of the bar was occupied by a signed photograph of his hero, and Rab spent many an hour regaling anyone who would listen with a story of how he had come by the photograph.

Kenny paused for a few seconds taking in the photograph and remembering how distraught Rab had been when Adamson had taken his own life. How he had closed the bar for a week and had not been seen out and about. Now that is a true fan, Kenny thought, before turning back to his beer.

Five

"Good beer."

Kenny was pulled back from his musings and felt someone standing next to him. He turned and looked straight at the guy who had been nursing the Irish whisky.

"Yes, yes, it is." Kenny stuttered back, taken aback that the man would speak to him.

But the man made no further comment. Instead he held up his empty tumbler and shook the melting ice to grab Rab's attention.

"Another please." The stranger requested.

Rab took a fresh glass from the shelf, filled it with a double Jameson's and placed it and an ice bucket in front of the stranger.

"I'll keep a tab." Rab said.

"Sure." Came the reply as the stranger put some ice in his glass which he then picked up before returning to his table.

"Was that an American accent?" Kenny whispered to Rab.

"Reckon so." Came the reply.

"How the hell did he come by here?" Kenny asked.

"No idea but he drinks a lot and pays well so I frankly don't give a damn."

Kenny held up his empty bottle indicating a refill was in order and glanced across to the American who seemed once again to be deep in thought staring into his glass.

Rab placed a second beer in front of Kenny and they both settled back into their own worlds.

The American too settled into his.

Six

Kenny was on his third beer before he heard the front door open and let in any new punters. He looked up as Sheila and Graham Walker entered. More locals, more regulars. Seemed to Kenny like only regulars drunk in The Hill.

Kenny nodded at Graham who ordered his drinks whilst Sheila took her seat in another booth.

"Hi." He said.

"Hi Kenny, how's things?" Graham asked.

"He's American." Kenny answered, nodding across to where the stranger was seated.

Graham looked over too.

"Oh, right." He answered before collecting his drinks and walking across to his wife, leaving Kenny alone once again.

Kenny went back to his beer and disappeared into his own world, a world where he felt safe and free from Goodman.

He glanced around again taking in the memorabilia again and paused at a framed photograph which seemed larger than most of the others. Kenny strained to see who it featured.

"Steve Windwood." The American again.

Kenny turned to see the anonymous American standing next to him again, clutching his tumbler and waiting for a refill.

"This guy can certainly drink." Kenny thought.

"Oh, right. Not someone I know about." He replied.

"Great vocalist and musician." The American went on, "Had his first number one when he was just fifteen with the Spencer Davis Group. You may have heard of it, Keep on Running."

"Can't say I have." Kenny replied.

"I have it on the Wurlitzer. I'll put it on." Rab was there at the bar again, ready with the Americans next drink.

Rab turned to leave and select the record and the American returned to his table without another word. Kenny drank some more.

Keep on Running came out from the speakers of Rab's old Wurlitzer, sitting as it did in pride of place at the end of the bar furthest from the door. Kenny glanced across at the marvelous old piece of musical machinery and wondered about a time before the streaming of music. It was certainly a wonderful piece of furniture and Rab clearly loved it because he never failed to engage in conversation about it, whenever the chance presented itself.

"It's a Wurlitzer 1050 you know." Kenny heard Rab say.

"So, you've said before." He replied.

Rab ignored the sarcasm in Kenny's voice.

"Only made sixteen hundred back in nineteen seventy-one. Got to be worth a few bob now you know."

"For sure."

"Takes a hundred old style forty fives."

Kenny lifted his empty beer bottle nodding at Rab for another, hoping he'd stop talking about his bloody jukebox. Kenny had heard it so many times before, he reckoned he could reel off the facts as easy as Rab did.

Rab did not take the hint. He turned to get the next beer for Kenny, but kept talking at the same time.

"Seen one for eight and a half grand just last year. Not as good condition as mine so it must be worth ten at least." He said.

"Sell the bloody thing then." Kenny came back, instantly regretting the tone of his voice. Rab didn't seem to notice, lost as he was in the love for the ancient Wurlitzer.

"If I played all the forty-fives one after the other, I could get five hours of non-stop music. Better than any new-fangled iPad thingy."

Kenny smiled, "I doubt that Rab, those can go on forever."

Rab shook his head, "Yeah but they ain't got the flashing lights have they?" He said.

Kenny smiled again. He'd never convince Rab about new technology. Old style vinyl and jukeboxes would win out every day with him. He gave up, yet again, and settled back with his beer.

Seven

Time moved on and the beers came as often as they were asked for. The music continued unabated too. Only anything Rab liked though. Requests could come but only those that had the Rab seal of approval were played. So, no Boyzone or Take That, and certainly no Girls Aloud or Little Mix.

In fact, not a lot from the twenty-first century at all. Maybe a little Bublé because he was a swinger at times, as was Robbie Williams and in a soft moment Rab even played Ed Sheeran and the occasional Adele, but mostly his choice of music came from artists who were at their peak between nineteen fifty and nineteen ninety. Mind you Kenny could put up with that.

The hours passed unnoticed as Kenny settled into a drinking rhythm and he hardly spoke to any of the other customers as they came and went. Mind you even at its busiest the bar that evening had no more than half a dozen punters. Kenny wondered how Rab kept the place going sometimes. Often though that he must have a secret income or a mass of savings stashed away somewhere. Rab never said.

The American hardly said another word as he kept up his regular saunter to the bar for a refill, and after a while Kenny hardly noticed him anymore and few words were exchanged.

Half way through Fleetwood Mac's Black Magic Woman, Kenny glanced at the clock over the bar.

"Shit." He muttered to himself as he saw it was already ten thirty.

"Where had four hours gone?" He thought to himself.

Same old story. Hours lost to drinking, never to be taken back. Were they really lost hours as his Mother had said, or was he actually enjoying himself, engaged in his one true hobby?

Some people spent a mini fortune on soccer matches, following their team all over the place win or lose. Others went to the cinema or smoked. Kenny drank. Why was that looked upon by some as a sin, a vice? Wasn't following a losing sports team a sin?

There were alcoholics but were there soccerholics? Who decided that one form of entertainment was OK after all and that another was tantamount to being an illness?

In the scheme of things Kenny's vice hurt no one. Bloody hell he knew married men who squandered a huge amount of their wages on going to football matches whilst their wives and kids suffered at home eating fish fingers and baked beans for dinner. But they weren't told to follow the twelve steps, were they? Not a chance.

Football was the "Beautiful Game", a national treasure but drinking was a vice, an illness to be frowned upon. But Kenny hurt nobody by drinking. No one went without because of him spending money on a few bottles of imported American IPA.

And he never, ever drove after a session. That was a golden rule he always followed. Quite apart from the fact that if he lost his license, he would lose his job, it wasn't right. Kenny knew that after a few beers his reaction time was shot to buggery. Recognised that fact and never wavered from his golden rule. No driving even after one beer.

He lifted the last bottle to his lips. Even after four hours it tasted good. But Toni's Pizzeria closed at eleven and he'd promised himself one of Toni's four meat monsters tonight. As he downed the last of his beer, he could almost taste the meat. Chrorizo, Parma ham, chicken and beef on top of a beautiful thin crust pizza topped with melted cheese, onions, peppers and homemade tomato paste.

Kenny placed the empty bottle of the bar and waved to Rab who was concentrating on what song would follow Peter Green's dulcet tones. He looked up at Kenny and walked to his note book by the till.

"Fourteen IPA's that's thirty-eight fifty. Call it thirty-five for cash HP." He said as he faced Kenny and held out his hand for the money.

"Is it really fourteen?" Kenny questioned even knowing that it was. Rab was never wrong.

"Sure was HP. You just kept on going tonight."

Kenny nodded in submission, handing over four ten-pound notes and silently promising to ease up tomorrow. He always promised to ease up tomorrow. But he knew he wouldn't. Rab took the notes and handed back Kenny's change.

"Same again tomorrow HP?" He asked.

Kenny nodded.

He made his way towards the door and glanced back as he did so to where the American still sat, nursing another Jameson's. The American raised the glass towards Kenny and tilted it his way in mock salute. Kenny nodded. No words were spoken. A silent acknowledgement of one drinker to another. Although they had never met before it seemed that they both knew they would meet again, most probably in The Hill tomorrow.

Kenny was smiling to himself as he turned and pushed the door open, feeling the chill of an English late evening as he began his walk home, stopping as planned at Toni's for yet another pizza to be eaten at home alone, most probably accompanied by yet more beers.

Meanwhile the American drunk on alone.

Eight

It had been almost midnight on Friday before Kenny had eventually found his bed. Most of the pizza had been eaten along with three more beers as Kenny watched yet more mindless, late night TV.

Saturday panned out as most Saturdays did for Kenny.

He woke about seven, rose fifteen minutes later and made the first of many coffees. It had been many years since he had suffered a hangover in spite of the level of alcoholic intake he maintained, so coffee was followed by toast and a look at the early morning TV news.

A second coffee followed around eight and then he tidied away the detritus of the previous evening. Bottles found their rightful place in the blue re-cycle bin whilst the empty pizza box was destined for another.

Kenny may have been well on the way to becoming an alcoholic, may have even reached that stage already, but he was not a slob, so he cleaned his small apartment, showered and dressed all by nine when the kettle produced his third coffee of the morning.

By nine fifteen Kenny was at a loss as to what to do next. He never, no rarely, drunk in the morning so he left his stock of beers well alone. In the absence of work his day was pretty empty. He had no close friends to call upon and followed no sporting activity, so physical exertion was not on the agenda. Instead he put on his wax jacket and ventured out.

First stop was the newsagents where he bought The Times. Then with it safely tucked under his arm, he ventured along the main street of his home town heading for the local convenience store.

An hour later Kenny was back at home reading his newspaper with yet another coffee.

By midday the paper was history and the remnants of Kenny's day stretched like a vacant playing field in front of him. A playing field without players. Without real purpose.

As he sat with coffee number six, or was it seven, he toyed with the idea of collecting his car but decided it was safer where it was in the car park of The Hill. It would probably stay there until he retrieved it Monday morning as he set off for work. Embarking on yet another futile five days of searching for sales that rarely if ever materialized.

He flicked through the channels on his TV settling on an old edition of a quiz show he had forgotten then name of, hosted by a long-forgotten celebrity host. As he watched he realized why the show was no longer aired. It was crap!

The afternoon dragged slowly on, as mindless TV was interrupted only by Kenny devouring the cold remnants of last night's pizza and downing yet more coffee.

By four Kenny's mood had gone through a number of phases. He had been entertained to a degree by an old episode of Life on Mars, and caught up with the latest world happenings on SKY news.

Then he had drifted off into a world of solemn melancholy as he recalled friends long since departed. Not in a *"now they are dead"* way, but in a *"don't want to socialize with Kenny"* type way.

Kenny tried to analyze why he had no friends as such. Was it because he drank? He didn't think so. Maybe it was his job. Nothing interesting to talk about there. But plenty of people had boring jobs. No that wasn't it.

On the other hand, maybe it was because most of them had settled down, got married and had kids, so much so that now he had absolutely nothing in common with any of them.

Sure, if they passed in the street there would be the usual chat.

"Hey Kenny, great to see you pal, let's catch up for a beer sometime." Or,

"You must come over some day join us for dinner."

None of it was genuine though. No plans ever came to fruition. In fact, no telephone numbers were exchanged so how could plans possibly be made, let alone completed.

By five Kenny had done all the usual soul searching and had come to the same conclusion he always did. None of it was his fault. It was because everyone else had deserted him, and safe in that knowledge he showered and dressed for the evening. Nothing posh mind. No need for that down The Hill, jeans and a rugby shirt would do.

No thought of meeting someone, of striking up a new relationship that warranted him dressing up to impress. Instead he would chat again with Rab and maybe one of the other regulars whilst slowly drinking away his worries and insecurities listening to Rab's eclectic choice of music.

As he walked back towards The Hill, Kenny allowed himself some positive thoughts.

Was his such a bad life? He had no debt. No loans or credit cards. No one who relied upon him to be a certain type of person or do certain things, to behave in a certain way. No, he had only himself to answer to and for, and that was a position that many of his former friends would love to be in. Or so he told himself as he walked along.

But somehow all of that didn't make things right. He was lacking purpose, something to strive for, a reason to be alive.

"Snap out of it, Kenny old mate." He admonished himself. "Brooklyn round the corner. Life's grand."

Truth be told by the time he opened the front door of The Hill around six that Saturday evening, Kenny had yet again convinced himself that all was well in the Jones household. So much so that it was with a slight smile on his face that he greeted Rab and took the first sip of his Brooklyn East India IPA.

"What's with you HP? Why the smile?" Rab asked as he made a note on his pad that Kenny had taken his first beer.

"Can't a man smile?" Kenny responded.

"Not in my boozer." Rab came back, laughing at his own joke.

"Yeah, there is that." Kenny replied, "Any chance of any decent music tonight?"

Rab turned away, back to his tasks muttering "Piss off," as he did so.

Kenny smiled to himself and for the first time noticed that the American was back in the same spot he had occupied the night before.

"Hey Rab." Kenny whispered. "He been there all night?" He asked as he nodded in the American's direction, trying to be subtle.

Rab approached and leant his face towards Kenny, presumably so that the subject of their conversation was ignorant to what was being said.

"Stayed 'til nearly midnight. Spent best part of hundred quid." He whispered.

"Bloody hell!" Kenny exclaimed.

"Exactly. Best customer I think I have ever had." Rab added.

"Is he local now?" Kenny asked, "Moved in somewhere?"

"That's what I was wondering but seems he is staying up at the B and B along Middle Street." Rab explained.

"Oh right. So, on holiday." Kenny observed.

"Dunno." Rab replied, "He's not one for chatting much, bit of a misery really, but he knows his music though. Got me to play some stuff I had forgotten about."

"Like what?" Kenny asked, all at once interested in the stranger and his music tastes. Anything to brighten up an otherwise boring Saturday evening, something new to talk about.

"The bloody Flying Burrito Bothers for God's sake. Thought only I had even heard of them buggers."

"Whoa, that takes a bit of doing Rab." Kenny came back, suitably impressed by the American's knowledge.

"That's not all. Even knew about Gram Parsons and Chris Hillman, rolled off a few songs of theirs that even I had forgotten. Damn impressive."

Kenny took another mouthful of beer. It was rare to see Rab this animated, and even more so to be impressed by another person's musical knowledge.

Kenny sensed someone behind him and his thoughts were interrupted by the American as he approached the bar with an empty glass. He raised it and Rab took it, turning to refill it without asking.

Kenny turned to look at the stranger and for the first time really looked at his face, taking it the features which he had previously largely ignored.

The guy was actually quite handsome, in a middle-aged man sort of a way, Kenny thought. He had a weathered yet friendly look about him and Kenny found himself wanting to say something, to draw him into a conversation. Something Kenny rarely wanted to do with anyone he didn't know.

"You impressed the crap out of old Rab hear apparently." He found himself saying.

Nine

The American looked over at Kenny, and for a moment Kenny thought he had overstepped the mark by speaking. It must have shown in his face.

"Been a while since I impressed any folks." The American replied.

Kenny took his cue and continued.

"Maybe so, but Rab loves people who like his sort of music and you knowing about the Flying Taco's was something that surprised him sure enough."

"Burritos." The American replied.

Kenny looked at him with a vacant look on his face.

"Burrito Bothers not Taco." The American clarified. "Wrong food."

Rab had approached with the Jameson's refill.

"Excuse this heathen will ya, he knows diddly squat about music." Rab added.

Kenny scowled as the American smiled.

"Like most folk, like most." He muttered as he turned and walked back towards what was swiftly becoming *"His Seat".*

Kenny growled at Rab, "No need for that you arsehole." He said. Rab just smiled and returned to cleaning glasses that might never be used.

Time moved on.

Six became seven and then eight o'clock fast approached. The American and Kenny seemed to be keeping pace with each other, not that either was openly keeping count. By eight both had had half a dozen each of their chosen poison.

The odd word had been exchanged as they came into close contact at the bar, but nothing of any great importance.

"He's looking a bit depressed don't you think?" Rab observed as he served Kenny yet another beer.

"Not sure I'd know." Kenny replied.

Rab smiled, "Sure you would HP, you're a bloody depressive bastard yerself."

"No, I am not. I'm just not all happy, smiley like a lot of people." Kenny came back with. "I'm what you'd call a depressive optimist." He added.

"Piss off HP. You're a definite glass half empty sort of a guy." Rab countered.

Kenny took another swig of his beer, finished the bottle.

Rab turned to fetch another from the cold cabinet.

"No thanks Rab." Kenny said, stopping the barista in his tracks.

"What? You off early?" Rab asked.

"No way." Kenny said, "But I think I'll have a Jim Beam and coke instead. I feel like a change."

Rab stopped still, surprised at the change in Kenny.

"Bugger me." He said, "Last time you did that you got well pissed and insulted Graham Walker's missus. What was it you called her? A shriveled-up hag."

"No, I merely said she wasn't looking good for her age." Kenny corrected.

Rab laughed out loud, "Yeah but you put it a little more bluntly than that. Had to stop Graham from putting one on yer." He said.

Kenny couldn't help but laugh and didn't hear the American approach for another refill.

"Sounds like we got a bit in common buster." He said to Kenny as they both waited for their drinks.

"Well if you get drunk and insult people, have no friends and are in denial about being close to becoming an alcoholic, then you and HP here are like blood brothers." Rab said as he served them both.

"Well add a bit about being a little fed up with life and maybe we'd be twins." The American added as he took his drink and returned to his seat.

Kenny picked up his new drink and took a large swig, feeling the burning sensation as it went down, a sensation that beer never provided. It felt good.

Rab nodded towards the American, "Go talk to him HP." He said.

"Now why would I do that?" Kenny asked as he turned and faced Rab.

"Sounds like you and he may have a bit in common, and sounds like he may have the need for someone to talk to or at least listen to what he wants to say." He added.

Kenny turned from Rab and looked across at the American, who was by then staring deeply into his glass. Kenny felt a jab of recognition. Felt that he saw in the American a lot of what he saw in himself. He put his glass to his lips and downed the remnants in one mouthful. Setting the glass down on the bar he turned towards Rab.

"Give me another and one for our cousin from over the sea too. Make them large ones." He said.

Ten

Kenny couldn't remember the last time he'd actually bought someone in The Hill a drink. It wasn't because he was tight or anything like that. No, it was because he rarely if ever, got into an exchange of rounds with anyone.

As he picked up the two glasses from the bar he paused, considered if what he was doing was right. He turned and saw Rab watching. Then Rab inclined his head slightly, urging Kenny on. Kenny turned and looked at the American who he was sure had not even noticed that he was going to approach.

"Sod it HP do it." Rab whispered.

Kenny was caught between a rock and a hard place. He was totally unused to being sociable and yet something was drawing him to the stranger. He felt something was sending him to the man, something he could not control. But his persistent fear of rejection held him back.

It was like he had two miniature people on his shoulders. A devil on one and an angel on the other, each either urging him on or holding him back. Normally the devil would win and he'd shy away from personal contact, but this time the angel seemed to be holding sway and he stepped towards the American's table.

As Kenny neared the table the American glanced up.

"I got you a refill." Kenny stuttered, holding out the fresh Jameson's.

No smile but the American did speak, "Mighty kind of you, but don't go gettin' any fancy ideas that it buys you a seat at my table." He said.

Kenny nodded, accepting yet another rebuke, in a long line of social put downs. He half turned making to walk away.

"Ah shit." He heard the American say.

Kenny turned back to face him.

"Sorry?" He said.

"I said shit." The American replied.

"Yes, I know. I heard that." Kenny said back and turned towards the bar again.

"Wait up buster, I didn't mean nothin', it's just me being a miserable bum again." The American said.

Kenny turned back and faced him, "No worries. I get like that too, so I understand. Enjoy your drink."

"I will." Came the reply, "Maybe you can enjoy yours too, sat here." The American said pointing towards the chair opposite him.

Kenny paused unsure. Should he politely decline and go back to solo drinking, or would that appear rude. He was torn, not used to such decisions. In the end he gave in and pulled out the chair and sat.

He raised his glass, "Cheers." He said.

Eleven

"Seems we're a lot alike, you and me." The American said.

Kenny sipped at his drink trying to settle himself, after all it had been a long time since someone, anyone, well anyone apart from Rab, had actually chosen to talk to him. Most times he was spoken to, or rather at, when he was sitting at the bar and was in someone's way. This was a whole new ball game.

"How so?" He replied.

The American looked hard into Kenny's eyes, which made him feel a little uncomfortable, but Kenny held that stare.

"Looks like we are fond of a drink or two for a start." He replied.

"Just to be sociable." Kenny replied defensively.

"Sure bud, just being sociable." Came the reply accompanied by a wry grin. "Four hours of sociability."

Kenny took the chance to glance towards the bar and caught Rab watching. "Definitely trying to hear what we're saying." Thought Kenny as he turned back to face the American.

"Where you from?" Kenny asked, knowing nothing else to say.

"Little place called Denton."

"Never heard of it."

"Don't doubt that. Even in Texas where it's at not many know of it."

"So how come you're here?"

The American paused, looking a little lost in thought.

"I ask myself that question a lot lately." He replied.

"And how do you answer yourself?"

The American smiled, "Now that Kenny boy is a dammed good question. You ain't as stupid as Rab says you are."

Kenny turned and shot Rab a hard stare. Rab caught the meaning if not the reason and raised his hands slightly as if asking "What?" Kenny turned back to his drink and the American.

"Don't go taking offense son." He said, "I reckon you are his best friend even if he don't recognise that."

Kenny took another swallow of his drink.

"Well if it's such a good question then what's the answer?" He asked.

"Best ways to tell it is that maybe I'm trying to lose myself and this is as good a place as any to do that."

"Why do you want to be lost?"

The American paused again, which seemed to be his habit as he contemplated his answer to Kenny's questions. Kenny was a patient guy, he could wait. He finished his drink and turned to Rab as the American remained silent. Kenny raised his glass with one hand and two fingers with the other. Rab nodded. Two more drinks were on their way. The American remained silent. When he broke his silence what he said saddened Kenny.

Twelve

The American paused as Rab approached with more drinks.

"My tab." Said Kenny. Rab nodded and the American didn't argue. Rab paused then turned and returned to the bar. Again, Kenny and the American were alone. Kenny waited. It seemed the right thing to do. Kenny wasn't blessed with many of the world's social graces but he had learned through bitter experience when to keep quiet. So, he remained silent and waited.

The American picked up his fresh drink and downed it in one.

"The bottle please barkeep." He said in Rab's direction, "And the same for my friend here." He added nodding at Kenny. Rab nodded too.

"Coming right up pal." He said and turned back to his shelf of drinks. He must have thought Christmas and his birthday had come at once. Surely, he had never made so much out of one customer before.

The American looked straight at Kenny, his eyes met Kenny's and Kenny saw sadness there. Sadness that he recognized often as he looked in his mirror in the morning as he shaved. He recognized in that moment a kindred spirit but again thought it best to remain silent. Some thoughts are best kept to yourself, he mused. The American seemed to read his mind.

"You are wise to say nothing." The American said, "Sometimes that is when the most is said." He continued.

He paused as Rab approached with a tray. Slowly and very precisely Rab placed an unopened bottle of Jameson's and another of Jim Beam on the table. Then followed six small, glass bottles of coke and a bucket of ice. He paused and the American spoke.

"My tab." He said simply. Rab acknowledged the American's request then he turned and went back to work. Kenny could see he wanted to hear what was being said, but he also saw that Rab knew when it was better to remain in the background.

Silence fell across the table interrupted only by the sound of the American pouring a fresh drink and adding two cubes of ice. He swilled his new drink, clinking the ice cubes together, then took a first sip.

"Drink shouldn't taste so good." He said. "If it didn't folks like us would take less."

Kenny smiled slightly, "But we like to drink, don't we?" He said.

"We sure do." Came the reply, "Don't make it right though."

Kenny had no reply to that.

"You gonna tell me your name then?" The American asked, "I sure as hell don't think it's HP."

"Kenny." Kenny replied, "Kenny Jones."

"Like the drummer." Said the American.

"Yeah, my Dad was a Faces fan."

"Good sound."

"I guess."

A short silence descended as they both took sips from their respective glasses. Temporary friends joined together in a common cause. Drinking.

"What about you?" Kenny asked, "You got a name?"

"We all got a name."

"And?"

"Hank. After Williams. My Dad was a fan."

"Before my time I think." Kenny suggested, as he had never heard of anyone called Hank Williams.

"Guess so." Came the reply. "Kinda fits the bill now."

"What does?"

"Being named after Hank Williams."

"How's that?"

"Hank died young, beat me to it far as that's concerned, but he wrote some real sad songs. Long Gone Lonesome Blues, Lost Highway, Wedding Bells. All songs about loves lost and having a pretty miserable life."

The American paused as if deep in thought.

"And then I'll Never Get Out of This Life Alive. Well that just about says it all, don't yer think Kenny?"

Kenny stared hard at his new if temporary friend and again saw true sadness.

"Don't know the lyrics but if the titles are anything to go by, I reckon your man Hank Williams was a pretty depressed guy."

The American sighed.

"Maybe he was but he certainly lived in tough times and I guess he just wrote it as he saw it."

"So why do you say you're like him?" Kenny asked.

Again, a silence fell on the table as the American carefully considered his response.

"Hank had it all, fame, a fortune of sorts by the standards of those days. But deep down I think he was unfulfilled."

"And are you unfulfilled?" Kenny asked.

The American laughed, but it wasn't a humorous laugh, more an ironic one Kenny thought.

"Hell, yes I reckon I am." Came the reply.

"How so?"

"Well I had a lot one time. Good career, the love of a woman I didn't come close to deserving. But I blew it as you Brit's say."

Kenny sipped his drink and waited for the American to continue, but he didn't. He seemed to withdraw into himself so Kenny let him.

Kenny fidgeted on his chair, a little uneasy and thought about taking his bottle and going back to the bar. The American again seemed to sense what Kenny was thinking and started to speak again, causing Kenny to settle back in his seat.

Thirteen

"Man, I should have been happy, but I wasn't. Always seeing the darkness instead of the light. That damn light at the end of the tunnel they all go on about. Well to me that was the light of an upcoming train, hurtling down the track to take me out." The American said, a sadness creeping into his narrative.

Kenny sat immobile, completely lost for any reply.

"How old are you son?" Hank asked.

"Thirty-five." Kenny replied.

"Thirty-five, thirty-five. Nice age. Know how old I am?"

Kenny looked hard at the American, trying to see past the obvious pain that had maybe aged him too early. He stabbed at a guess,

"Fifty." He said, hoping he would flatter rather than insult. Secretly he had thought that the American might be sixty. He looked it.

The American laughed.

"Trying to be polite hey?" He said.

Kenny blushed slightly but didn't reply, just grinned a little.

"Hell, boy I am just ten years older than you. Forty-five this month."

Kenny couldn't help but show his surprise.

"Ain't worn too well. Let that be a lesson Kenny boy. Too much fretting and drinking can do that to yer."

"I suppose it can. But I don't fret that much." Kenny replied.

"Bullshit!" Hank blasted, so much so that Rab looked up from the book he was reading behind the bar.

"I can see you fret nearly as much as I do. And as for drinking, well lookey there at the bottle in front of you. Getting on to being half empty."

Kenny blushed again and was taken aback by the American's accurate assessment.

Kenny knew he was a drinker. Been on one of those alcoholic's sites and done a questionnaire, and even though he had lied when answering some questions, it had come back that he exhibited an eighty percent propensity towards becoming an alcoholic. Kenny had dismissed it but the American was bringing it all back to him now.

And as for fretting as the American put it, well Kenny was the world's worst at stressing himself over almost anything.

"Got you thinking, huh?" Hank asked.

Kenny was shaken back to reality from his thinking about the past, but he didn't answer.

"Makes no difference whether you admit to it or deny it to yourself. It is what it is. You ain't gonna make it go away by ignoring it or denying it." The American stated.

"But this isn't about me." Kenny said harshly.

"Maybe not, maybe it is." Came the reply.

Both sipped some more and topped up their glasses. Hank broke the silence.

"Goddam gone and lost my woman." He said, "Got the papers last week. She wants shot of me."

"Sorry to hear that." Was all Kenny could think to say.

"Career shot to hell too."

"Can either be saved?" Kenny asked.

"Why?" Came the reply.

"Well because if both were worth having once then they are worth having again maybe."

Hank looked across at Kenny, considering what he had just said. He drunk some more before responding.

"Maybe you're right but somethings just can't be gotten back." He said.

"Maybe not but you don't know unless you give it a go."

"Well ain't you the little psychiatrist."

"Just saying what I think." Kenny replied defensively.

"Yeah well I reckon I done all the fighting at getting things back that I got in me. Now all that saves me is in that there bottle of whisky." The American said, pointing at the bottle before him as he did so.

Kenny looked at the bottle in front of the American which was emptying fast. Then he looked at the one in front of him and saw that it too was nearer empty than full.

Then he looked at the American, at Hank, and saw not just a worn out American, but also a possible look into a future that lay in store for him. It shook him to think that he was heading the same way.

"So, if you're giving up the fight what is left?" He asked.

"Nuttin'." Came the reply, "Ain't nuttin' left for me in this world old buddy."

"So how do you live with that?" Kenny asked.

"Maybe I decided that I ain't gonna." Came the stark reply.

Kenny's mouth fell open a little as he took in what had just been said.

Surely this guy didn't mean that he's going to top himself, he thought. Nah, I misread that.

Fourteen

"Didn't mean to shock you none." The American said, "Just saying how it is."

Kenny wanted to take the conversation away from where it had headed so he tried to change the subject. Like most people the question of suicide was one that scared the shit out of him.

He'd thought about it himself oddly enough. Once, when things were really on top of him. But he'd not had the balls to see it through. Or at least that's what he told himself. In the end he had decided that it actually took more balls not to do it, than to go ahead. Took more strength to overcome his dark feelings than to give in to them.

And overcome it he had. Clearly, he still drank too much but what the heck, one problem at a time.

"So, you on holiday here then, to sort your head out?" He asked.

The American looked up and laughed. Not out loud but he laughed none the less.

"Who the hell comes to this God forsaken place for a holiday boy?" He asked.

"It's not that bad." Kenny responded a little defensively.

"Sorry son, didn't mean to insult your home town. Shit where I come from ain't no picture-perfect place neither."

Kenny held up a hand in mock surrender.

"No offence taken. Well if not a holiday then what?" He enquired.

"Wanted to be some place I ain't known, I guess. Didn't want no person prying, certainly didn't want no person who might know me, well you know, finding me."

Once again Kenny was drawn back to the question of suicide. Surely, he had misread things, that can't be what the American was meaning. Surely no one spoke openly about ending their life. Not with a total stranger.

The American again broke him from his thoughts.

"I know what you're thinking son." He said. "Maybe I talk too much sometimes when I get to drinking. Don't pay me no mind."

"I get lonely too sometimes." Kenny said.

"This ain't just lonely." The American came back with. "This is much more than that."

"Yeah, well maybe I know that too. Been there too." Kenny replied.

No reply from the American. He just poured another drink.

"Been down so far sometimes that I saw no way back up, but I hung in there and, well, here I am."

The American went to speak but Kenny surprised himself by cutting him off.

"I know what you're thinking. Where I am isn't such a great place to be. Yeah you may be right. It may not be such a great place what with the drinking and everything." Kenny took a deep breath and, ironically, another drink. "But it's where I am right now. One thing dealt with, one more to go. Small steps, but steps forward none the less."

Kenny sat back for a second, proud of what he was saying. He rarely opened up to anyone over how he felt and yet here he was doing exactly that with a total stranger. Maybe it was easier with someone who you may well not see again after tonight. It gave him the strength to carry on.

"You got money?" He asked.

The American shook his head, "Sure I got money."

"Well there you go." Kenny retorted.

"There you go what?" Hank asked back.

"One plus in your favour." Kenny replied, "One nil to Hank." He said and laughed at his own joke. Well an almost joke.

Fifteen

"Money don't mean much when there's no one to share it with." Hank said.

"Yeah I know what they say, money can't buy you happiness." Kenny came back with, "But no poor man ever said that did they?"

The American laughed again, "That's true enough, easy to say you don't need it when you got it, I guess."

"Exactly, I'd sure like to try and see what having a few quid more would do to my life. In the scheme of things, it seems that it might be easier to be miserable when you're rich than when you're poor." Kenny responded.

The American smiled again, "You got a point there, son." He said. "But money on its own is not enough."

"You married?" Kenny asked, switching the subject.

"For the moment yeah, I'm married."

"For the moment?" Kenny questioned.

"Seems she don't feel I am a good person to be around. Filed for divorce just last week."

"Is that why you're here?" Kenny asked.

The American took another sip of whisky and seemed to be pondering his reply. Kenny drank some more too, as he waited.

"Maybe it is." The American eventually replied.

"So, you ran away." Kenny said, and immediately regretted being so harsh as the American shot him a glance that could have cut him down.

"You got no right to judge me boy." The American said.

Kenny leant back I his chair.

"I wasn't judging. Look maybe I worded that wrong. I didn't mean running away, maybe I meant were you trying to get some place where you could think." He said, back tracking swiftly.

"No need to apologize, I shouldn't be so swift to judge." Came the reply.

"Well?" Kenny asked.

"It was space I needed in a way. To be away from where I'm known." The American said, appearing almost maudlin to Kenny. He thought it was sad to see.

"First and only woman I really loved you know. Kathy. That's her name. Short for Katherine."

The American paused and reached into his back pocket and extracted a beaten-up brown, leather wallet. He opened it and withdrew an old dog-eared monochrome photograph. He paused and looked longingly at the photograph before reaching over and handing it to Kenny.

"She loved black and white photography, felt it took her back to old times when life was simpler." The American said as if explaining why the photograph was recent but not in colour.

Kenn took the photo from the American and looked down at it. Staring back at him was the smiling face of quite the most beautiful woman Kenny had ever seen outside of a fashion magazine. Although the photograph was not in colour Kenny could tell she was a brunette and maybe about his own age.

"She is beautiful." Was all Kenny could think to say.

"She sure is Kenny." The American replied, using Kenny's name for maybe the first time. "That was taken maybe four years ago and she is now even more beautiful if that's at all possible. But I lost her."

"But you can get her back?" Kenny asked.

The American shook his head, "Not sure I can. She seems to have given up on me." He added.

"Or have you given up on yourself?" Kenny suggested, "And she can't live with that. Maybe if you believed in yourself, she would again. You ever thought of that?"

"Hell, I gave up on me long times ago. Seems that she only just realized that and joined me." Hank responded.

"Well that's a good sign." Kenny stated.

The American looked across at Kenny, confused.

"How you work that out?" He asked.

"Maybe she knew you'd thrown in the towel but stuck around hoping you'd change, hoping or trying to get you back to believing in yourself again. Then after a while she saw you weren't coming back so she too threw in the towel and gave up." Kenny replied.

"That's sure a new way to look at things." The American said.

"I seen it before." Kenny said, on a roll now. "My Father was an alcoholic."

"In your genes then." The American interrupted. Kenny ignored the jibe.

"My Mother tried so hard to help him through it. Nearly succeeded too. He was dry for five years then got laid off. Sent him back to the bottle. Only this time there was no bringing him back." Kenny continued.

The American drank some more but concentrated completely on what Kenny was saying.

"She tried, oh she bloody well tried." Kenny continued, "I was only about thirteen but I understood, could see what she was going through."

Kenny paused and poured another drink, noticing that the bottle was getting ever and ever closer to being empty. He couldn't remember ever drinking this much in one session and yet he didn't feel drunk. Was that a good or a bad sign he thought, before carrying on.

"Then one time he went AWOL for a whole weekend. She was at her wits end. Couldn't find him anywhere."

"He come back?" The American asked.

"Yes, he did." Kenny replied.

"And was it OK?"

"Hell no. As you Yanks would say." Kenny replied.

"And?"

"He was a wreck. Kept drinking and had given up completely."

"And she left him?" The American asked.

"Not at first. She battled on. Kept finding his bottles and emptying them so he couldn't drink. But he always had more somehow. Lasted maybe six months like that. It was like a living hell, walking on eggshells all the time."

"He hit her?"

"No never!" Kenny stated forcefully, "Never like that. He was just always angry. Not at us but at himself."

"What happened?" The American asked, and Kenny noticed that he seemed genuine in his interest, as if he recognized a similarity somewhere in his own and Kenny's lives.

"In the end she had to leave him. She packed up our things one day and drove off. Left him a note."

"What did it say?"

"Said she couldn't take any more, couldn't live with someone who didn't want to live with themselves. Said not to contact her unless he really wanted to change. Said if he did, she'd come back and help in that change.

She never really gave up on him, not completely. He just thought she had."

"And you think my Kathy is like your Mother?" Hank asked.

"Only one way to find out." Kenny replied.

"How's that?"

"Ask her."

Sixteen

After that the American seemed to sink back a little, became less talkative and more thoughtful, introspective.

For Kenny the night ended when the bottle did. No way would he ever think of drinking more after the bottle went dry.

Just before eleven he made his excuses and walked home.

Another stop, at Toni's for yet another pizza. Glad he just caught him as he prepared to lock up.

Back home, and much against his better judgement Kenny accompanied the pizza with a couple of beers and spent a long while sat in an easy chair contemplating what had happened in The Hill that night, thinking about what was said and wondering if the American, Hank, had really given up on life and if he was really contemplating suicide. Or was that just Kenny reading things all wrong. Wouldn't be the first time. Kenny tried to ease his conscience by telling himself it was the bottle talking. God knows it had talked to him often enough.

By the time he went to bed around one the next morning, Kenny had decided that he'd go to The Hill on Sunday and probably meet Hank again and all would be fine.

But he slept fitfully, dreaming of his parents and of the bit of their story he had not felt he could tell the American.

The bit where his Father killed himself.

Seventeen

Kenny woke early on Sunday morning and busied himself tidying up yet more empty beer bottles and pizza boxes, something he promised himself every Saturday and Sunday morning he would never do again. Just as well he had no one in his life after all, they'd certainly not put up with this early morning slovenliness.

By midday he'd had several cups of coffee, two slices of toast for breakfast and cleaned up and the place was looking good enough to accept visitors. But none would come. Kenny knew that, so he showered and made himself look half way presentable and set off into the world outside.

First stop was the newsagents where Kenny bought The Sunday Times. Sure, it cost almost three quid but it was big enough to see him through Sunday and Monday as far as reading was concerned. Oh, and it had a weekly TV guide too.

Newspaper safely tucked under his arm Kenny set off to The Hill.

For some reason Kenny didn't take the direct route. This time he detoured into Middle Street where his journey took him past the town's only bed and breakfast run by a spritely seventy-year-old woman Kenny knew only as Rita. The place he had been told by Rab that the American was staying.

Kenny had no idea why he went that way, and he had no intention of stopping. But as he passed, he allowed his gaze to venture upwards to the building's windows. He saw nothing and walked on.

By twelve-thirty he was pushing open the door to The Hill and smiling as Rab set his beer down upon the bar.

"You had a few last night." Rab observed.

Kenny nodded, "Funny enough it didn't seem to have any effect." He added.

"Not a good sign HP, not a good sign." Rab said as he turned to continue cleaning the bar.

Kenny settled into his normal Sunday morning ritual. Reading the Times and sinking a few beers.

That same ritual continued into the afternoon as he walked home via the local chippie where he filled up on haddock and chips.

More reading followed at home as did his Sunday evening stint at The Hill.

By the time he left the pub that evening Kenny had almost forgotten that the American had not shown up that day. Not at lunchtime nor the evening.

Eighteen

Monday started as normal with Kenny collecting his car from the car park at The Hill. It then continued as any other Monday with the early morning visit to the office to collect that week's client list.

There followed the normal eight hours of Kenny desperately trying to sell printer cartridges to unsuspecting customers and failing miserably. By the time he signed off with a call to the office around six that afternoon, Kenny's sales amounted to less than three hundred pounds. If he kept up that level of sales, he would barely hit his weekly target, let alone make enough for any bonus pay. Situation normal.

Normally Kenny didn't drink on a Monday. His one effort at proving to himself that he didn't actually need alcohol so he couldn't be an alcoholic. But oddly enough, as he approached The Hill on his way home, he seemed drawn to the bar.

He hadn't given the American any real thought during the day but as he pulled into the pub's car park, he felt himself wondering why he had not shown up at the place on Sunday.

Kenny pulled up in the otherwise empty car park. He placed his brief case in the boot out of sight of prying eyes and walked to the front door, where he hesitated slightly before pushing it open.

As he entered his eyes drew accustomed to the half-light and he saw Rab stood by his Wurlitzer selecting some music. He turned and stopped what he was doing when he saw Kenny.

"Bugger me HP. What the hell you doing here on a Monday?" He asked.

"What, don't you need the business?" Kenny came back with.

"Always good to see you, old son, just a bit of a surprise."

"Just fancied a quickie on the way home. Fed up doing the same thing every day." Kenny replied.

"OK. Let me guess the drink then. In case you're changing that too." Rab said with a chuckle.

Kenny raised his hand, stopping Rab in his tracks.

"Great idea Rab you old Scotch git." Kenny mocked.

"Scottish you English tosser. Scotch is a drink." Rab responded with a wide grin.

"In that case I will have…………" Kenny paused as he considered what to drink. "A bottle of Old Norway."

Rab smiled again, "Aye Orkney's best." He said and fetched a bottle of the rarely seen beer, which he placed along with a matching glass on the bar in front of Kenny.

"Seen the American?" Kenny asked after taking the first drink of his beer.

"Not seen him at all. He left after you Saturday, settling up his tab. No sign of him yesterday and today is too early." Rab said.

Kenny nodded knowingly and turned back to his beer whilst Rab finished loading selections on his Wurlitzer.

By eight Kenny had had enough and wandered home.

Still no sign of the American.

Nineteen

Tuesday and Wednesday followed suit but without the detour to The Hill and by Thursday Kenny had all but forgotten the American, but on the way home a rare song on the car radio featuring Gram Parsons, brought him back to mind.

With the song fresh in his mind Kenny pulled into the car park of The Hill and stepped inside for a drink.

"Well, well, twice in a week HP. Getting to be a bad habit." Rab observed.

Kenny looked around the pub as he approached the bar and saw no other customers.

"Looks like you could do with the trade." He quipped.

"Piss off." Came the response.

"Just heard a song on the radio reminded me of the American." Kenny said.

Rab's eyes twinkled.

"Oh yeah, which one?"

"In the Darkness by that Gram Parsons bloke. Did it with some bird." Kenny replied.

"In My Hour of Darkness, you heathen. And that bird as you put it was Emmylou Harris." Rab corrected.

"Whatever." Kenny retorted. "Anyway, reminded me of the American, so I thought I'd stop by. He been in?"

"Nope. Again, not a sign." Rab answered. "I guess he's moved on. Never was going to be a local ever."

"Guess not. Oh well he wasn't that bad a bloke when I got to chat with him. Bit depressive but OK." Kenny replied.

"Certainly knew his music." Rab added, "And he was a good spender."

Twenty

Kenny had no idea why and when questioned about it later could offer no explanation as to why later that night, he left his flat and wandered down to Rita's B & B in Middle Street. But he did.

"Hello Kenny." Rita said as he entered the front door and approached the small reception desk. "Don't see you here often."

"No, I suppose not but……" Kenny started but was interrupted.

"I'm guessing you've come about Hank." Rita said.

"Well yes. How do you know that?" Kenny asked Rita, totally taken aback for a moment.

"He said you would come to collect what he left for you. Said it was the one last thing he had to do. Leave this for you." Rita replied.

Kenny remained silent as Rita reached into a drawer and withdrew a small jiffy bag which she handed to Kenny.

"He gave me this when he left. Said you'd be over for it. Have to say I had expected you before now." Rita said.

"Sorry but I've been busy." Was all Kenny could think to say as he took the package, mumbled his thanks and stepped outside into the street.

So, the American, Hank, had gone. Kenny thought as he hurried from Rita's. He had gone a few yards before he even thought to look at the package he held in his hand.

Kenny stared at the neat handwriting on the front of the sealed jiffy bag,

It's been a long, long time coming, But I know a change gonna come. Sam

Kenny studied the words but they meant nothing to him. And who is Sam? The American said his name was Hank. What the heck Kenny thought as he unsealed the bag.

He looked inside and couldn't help let out an audible gasp. He closed it again and walked quickly home.

Once home Kenny set the jiffy bag down on the small dining table and fetched a beer from the fridge.

He was trembling as he sat and reached for the bag.

He paused and drank the whole bottle of beer, fetched another and sat staring at the bag again.

Surely, he had seen things wrong, he thought, when he looked inside the package outside Rita's. Yeah that's it.

Kenny nervously reached for the package again, staring once more at the writing on the front. The words that still meant nothing.

Tentatively he unsealed it once again and reached inside and withdrew the contents.

No, he hadn't been seeing things, it was full of American dollars.

It looked like more money that Kenny had ever seen in his life before. So, he nervously counted. There were five neat bundles, each secured with a paper wrap the kind banks put round bundles of notes.

Kenny counted carefully. Each bundle contained fifty, one hundred-dollar bills.

Kenny did the math's. Sat on his table was twenty-five thousand dollars in cash.

Kenny hurriedly took out his mobile phone and searched for a currency converter. He tapped in the amounts and froze. Sat on his table was a pile of dollars, worth a little more than twenty-thousand pounds.

Kenny finished his second beer and took another, trying to stop the shaking.

Why had the American left this with Rita? And why had she been asked to give it to him? What the hell should he do?

Kenny sat back, staring at the money on his table.

He drank a third then a fourth beer.

Then he had a eureka moment. He gathered up the money and put it back into the jiffy bag. He put on his jacket, stuffed the bag in an inside pocket and hurried to The Hill. Rab would know what to do.

Twenty-One

"Not you again?" Rab said as Kenny entered and rushed to the bar. "Come any more often and I'll have to get you yer own chair."

Then Rab stopped and stared at Kenny.

"What's got into you? Looks like you seen a ghost." Rab said to Kenny as he pulled up a stool at the bar.

"Give me a large Jack Daniels and coke." Kenny blurted out.

If Rab was surprised he didn't let it show. He just fetched the drink, sat it down in front of Kenny, stared at him and said,

"Well, you going to tell me what's got you in this flap?"

Kenny downed his drink in one mouthful, forgetting to add any of the coke. He slammed the glass down and nodded to Rab.

"Another please. And pour yourself something and then be quiet."

Rab knew when to remain silent so he did what Kenny asked. Then he waited.

"You seen the American since Saturday?" Kenny asked.

"I told you before. No." Rab replied.

"He's gone." Kenny stated.

"How you know that?"

"Just spoke to Rita."

"Now why would you do that?" Rab asked.

"I wish I knew." Kenny replied, "But I am glad I did because she gave me this."

Kenny withdrew the jiffy bag and laid it on the bar. Rab stared at it.

"What is that?" He asked.

"Rita said the American left it behind when he left." Kenny said.

"So why you got it?" Rab enquired.

"She said he left it for me." Kenny replied again.

"How'd you know it were there?"

"I didn't. I just passed by to see if he was there and Rita told me. He must have known I'd ask after him." Kenny said, as if that explained everything.

"Maybe so. But what's in it?" Rab enquired.

"Just a sec. Look at this first." Kenny said, turning the bag over so Rab could see the writing.

"The American said his name was Hank." Kenny started, "So why's this note from Sam?" He asked as he downed yet another full glass.

Rab read the words on the bag.

"It's not from Sam." He stated.

"But is says so." Kenny said, tapping the bag where the name Sam was clearly written.

Rab shook his head.

"You know nothing about music you idiot." He said.

Kenny looked bemused.

"It's not from Sam." Rab said, "Those are lyrics from a Sam Cooke song." He finished.

Kenny remained looking blank.

Rab tried to put him out of his misery.

"Those are two lines from the song A Change is Gonna Come." He said.

He then turned to the Wurlitzer and played the song. All at once things seemed to become clearer to Kenny and he silently thanked the strange American named Hank, who seemed to know all about music.

Twenty-Two

Kenny was nothing if not honest and, against Rab's advice, he had spoken to Brian the local beat copper. He also handed over the dollars from Rita's.

Word went up the line and Brian came back to Kenny a week later.

The money was legally Kenny's. He had said. And no, there was no news about the American.

No body had been found anywhere fitting his description so there was no reason to think anything had happened to him. Brian's boss was happy that he was just some eccentric Yank who had gone back to the States leaving behind a few quid to a one-time drinking buddy.

Kenny was not used to having money but he knew what he wanted to do, or rather he knew what he didn't want to keep on doing. So, he quit his job, used some of the money as a deposit on a better rented flat and looked around for a better job. He also bought a better car. Investments he called them, for his future.

Now almost a year later he still had over half of the money and although he hadn't found a good job as yet, he had hopes, with a recent interview under his belt and awaiting the result. For once he felt hopeful about the future.

Somethings never change though and Friday night saw him again in The Hill and, even though it was gone ten o'clock, he was the only customer when the door flew open and Graham Walker burst in.

"That desperate for a drink Graham?" Rab asked.

Graham rushed to the bar and pointed up to Rab's widescreen TV on the wall.

"That thing work?" He blurted out.

Rab looked offended.

"Course if bloody works. It's not for show." He retorted.

"Turn it on, turn it on to BBC One, get Graham Norton on."

"That Irish idiot. I don't think so." Rab replied.

"Just turn the bloody thing on." Graham shouted.

Rab took the hint and muttering under his breath he retrieved the remote control and turned on Graham Norton.

The screen came alive with Graham Norton sat in front of the normal sofa of guests. Graham waved his hand excitedly.

"There, there, look!" He shouted. Kenny had never seen him so animated.

"Who? Hugh Grant, so what?" He said.

"No, not him you dick! The bloke at the end." Graham shouted.

At that moment the camera closed in on Graham Norton and Hugh Grant so the other end of the sofa was lost for the moment.

"Shut up Graham and listen for a sec." Rab barked.

Silence fell across Rab and his two customers.

"Well then Hugh that's great news, when can we expect it to hit our screens?" Norton asked.

"Should be in two months, end of October, so look out." Grant replied.

"Well you heard it here first ladies and gents, from the horse's mouth so to speak."

Norton continued.

"Come on, come on, show the rest." Graham muttered.

Then the camera panned out so that the whole sofa was in view.

"He's gone!" Graham exclaimed as the camera revealed Hugh Grant and some female soap star who none of them recognized.

"You've lost it mate." Kenny observed.

"No, no wait listen up Norton's speaking again." He replied.

"And now to close the show a special treat and one that this time last year his many fans would have not thought possible. Bringing us his new single, his own version of the Sam Cooke classic A Change is Gonna Come, I give you the rejuvenated, Hank Jackson."

Cue much clapping as the camera swept to the right of the sofa and focused on the stage on which sat a lone man and his guitar.

"Holy shit!" Exclaimed Kenny.

"Jesus Christ!" Rab added. "It's the bloody American."

The camera zoomed in on the stage and silence fell both in The Hill and in the Graham Norton stage. Then the American spoke.

"Those that know me, and some that think they do, will know that it is nothing short of a miracle that I am here tonight." He started, in a low and intense voice, "Only a year ago I thought I had lost the one person who believed in me because I thought that she stopped doing just that. But she hadn't, it was me who had stopped believing in myself." He continued.

The American paused and seemed to gaze up into the audience. The camera man switched to the person that he was looking at and focused in on a pretty brunette, sitting alone in the crowd and smiling at the man on the stage, albeit a little self-consciously.

The woman from the photograph, Kenny thought to himself.

The camera held her in its gaze for a second before returning to the American who started to speak again.

"Then some stranger, a Brit of all people." He paused and smiled and the audience laughed with him, quietly.

"Well he taught me otherwise. No doubt he ain't got a clue what he did and unless he's watching this he may never know, but he made me think, made me see things differently, made me change my mind. And well here I am now 'cos of him. He listened. Not many folks know how to do that. Most just want to let you think they're listening when all they want to do is preach right back at you or even just leave you to it. Sometimes when you're down in the gutter you need someone to listen so you can see there's a reason to climb right back out. That's what this guy, this Kenny, did for me. He listened and when he spoke back, he weren't judging me, he was just telling me how he thought it was. And he was right."

The American paused and the audience acknowledged what he was saying with polite applause. Then they fell silence.

"No exaggeration when I say that if he hadn't listened then I wouldn't be here right now. I had made the choice to end it as I saw no way ahead that was good to see. What he said got me thinking and got me talking to Kathy again and got her talking to me again. And here we are now. So, Kenny, wherever you are this one's for you son."

The American paused, accepted the applause from the audience, set himself up with his guitar and delivered a heartfelt version of the great Sam Cooke classic.

In The Hill there was complete silence for the few minutes the song lasted. Then at the end the camera homed in on Kathy, Hank's wife and caught her with a tear in her eye, before focusing back on Hank for a few seconds before switching to Graham Norton who seemed genuinely moved when he simply said.

"And on that note, good night ladies and gentlemen."

Rab turned off the TV and looked at Kenny.

"What you drinking HP? My shout."

Printed in Great Britain
by Amazon

84733338R00057